THE SAD
GERANIUMS

By the same author

THE MAN OUTSIDE

Wolfgang Borchert

THE SAD GERANIUMS

and other stories

Translated by
Keith Hamnett

The Ecco Press
New York

Originally published in Germany
by Rowolt Verlag as
Die Traurigen Geranien

© Rowolt Verlag GmbH, Reinbeck bei Hamburg 1962
© This translation Calder & Boyars Ltd, London 1973

Published in 1973 in a hardbound and
paperbound edition by The Ecco Press
1 West 30th Street, New York, N.Y. 10001

SBN 912-94610-5 (hardbound)
SBN 912-94611-3 (paperbound)

Library of Congress Catalogue
Card Number: 73-11251

Printed in Great Britain by
Galliard (Printers) Ltd, Great Yarmouth

CONTENTS

INTRODUCTION

Wolfgang Borchert was born in Hamburg on 20 May, 1921, and died in a Basle nursing home on 20 November, 1947. After leaving school he worked first as a bookseller and then decided to become an actor. In 1941, aged 20, he was called up and sent to the Eastern front. Severely wounded in 1942 he was repatriated and in the same year he was arrested. His outspoken criticism of the Nazi régime made him a permanent suspect in the eyes of the authorities. On a charge of having uttered 'defeatist' remarks about the régime and thus having jeopardised the State he was sentenced to death. The sentence was, however, commuted to six months' solitary confinement on account of his youth. In 1944, after having been sent back to the Russian front, his health began to fail and he was discharged from the army.

Back in civilian life he appeared in various Hamburg theatres and cabarets. Once again he fell foul of the authorities with his satirical remarks in cabaret performances. This time he was given a nine months' prison sentence. When he was released in 1945 he was a broken, chronically sick man. He spent the next two years writing, in a feverish race against death precipitated by the war, imprisonment, jaundice, diphtheria and the deprivations of the immediate post-war years. By the time friends managed to raise the money for a cure in Switzerland it was already too late. He died the same year.

When he died, the day after the première of his play THE MAN OUTSIDE, his name became a household word in Germany and he was henceforth identified with this his major work. Borchert wrote the play—which he subtitled 'A play which no theatre will produce and no public will want to see'—in a few days in the late autumn of 1946.

His literary output was necessarily limited, yet it spanned a vast range of the emotions and revealed a disciplined, but none-the-less, passionate and sensitive artist whose commitment to the young and lonely continues to keep his name alive.

Borchert wrote about hopelessness, but was, nevertheless, for a short period of time, the only voice of hope in the wilderness. He was a solitary, an outsider, one who died young and so it is only natural that he should become the chosen idol of the disillusioned young in post-war shattered Germany. Yet, in his lifetime, he never considered himself as the exception. He never exalted the 'I', never stressed the victimization of the 'outsider' but spoke only of the collective suffering, the fate of the 'betrayed generation'. The fact that he absolved youth from all the burden of guilt at a time when guilt, especially collective guilt, was uppermost in every mind, undoubtedly sparked off his potential popularity.

The interpretation of the writer as 'herald of his time'—appropriate though this is in many respects—would appear to be only one facet of Borchert's talent when one considers the eighteen short stories collected in this volume. Here we are confronted with a writer of exceptional sensitivity, who is able to convey in the sparsest of sketches the extreme spiritual anxiety that lurks beneath the bland exterior.

This collection of stories was discovered among the papers of his estate. They were written in 1946 and 1947 and cover an astonishing range of mood and style. Some of them are fragments like *Dear, Blue-Grey Night*, a poetic dialogue between two young lovers, or *Behind the Windows it is Christmas*, which tells of the longing and loneliness of a soldier desperate to escape from barrack life, seeking the love of a girl to light up his Christmas. Sketchy some of the stories may be, but they conjure up a whole world of sad and lonely people with an imagery that is at once poetic, memorable and essentially relevant today.

THE SAD GERANIUMS

⟨∿∿⟩

They had met when it was dark. Then she had invited him and he had come. She had shown him her apartment and the tablecloths and the bed-linen and also the plates and forks she had. But now that they faced each other for the first time in broad daylight he could see her nose.

That nose looks as if it has been sewn on, he thought. And it doesn't look a bit like other noses. More like garden produce. Good heavens! he thought. And look at those nostrils! They are completely unsymmetrical. Their relationship to each other is devoid of harmony. One is narrow and oval. But the other gapes just like an abyss. Dark and round and unfathomable. He reached for his handkerchief and dabbed at the sweat on his brow.

"It's so warm, isn't it?" she began.

"Oh yes," he said, and looked at her nose.

Again he thought: it must be sewn on. It seems so out of place in her face. And it has a totally different tinge from the rest of her skin. Much more intense. And the nostrils really are without harmony. Or, it occurred to him, they have a completely original sort of harmony, as in a Picasso.

"Yes," he continued, "wouldn't you agree that Picasso is on the right track?"

"Who?" she asked, "Pi——ca——?"

"Well, maybe not," he sighed. Then, suddenly, without any transition: "You must have had an accident."

"Why do you say that?" she asked.

"Oh, well," he muttered helplessly.

"Ah, I see, because of the nose?"

"Yes, that's right."

"No, it's always been like that." She said it quite patiently. "That's how it has always been."

"Christ!" he nearly said. But all he said was "Oh, really?"

"And yet I am such a harmonious person," she whispered. "And how I love symmetry. Just look at my two geraniums on the window ledge. There's one on the right and one on the left—symmetrical. No, you must believe me, inwardly I am quite different. Quite different."

As she spoke she laid her hand on his knee and he could feel her horribly sincere eyes burn through to the back of his skull.

"And I also believe in marriage, in living together. Utterly," she said, in a soft, somewhat embarrassed tone of voice.

2

"It's the symmetry, isn't it?" he couldn't help saying.

"Harmony," she corrected him gently, "because of the harmony."

"Of course," he said, "harmony."

He stood up.

"Oh, you're leaving?"

"Yes, I—yes."

She showed him to the door.

"Inwardly I am really so different," she began again.

Yes, he thought, but your nose is an imposition. An imposition that has been sewn on. And he said out loud: "What you mean, inwardly you are like the geraniums. Perfectly symmetrical. Isn't that it?"

Then he went downstairs, without turning round.

She stood at the window and watched him go.

Then she saw him stop and wipe his brow with his handkerchief. Once, twice. And then once again. But she did not see the grin of relief spread over his face. That she did not see because her eyes had filled with tears. And the geraniums, they were just as sad. In any case, that's how they smelled.

LATE AFTERNOON

The house was narrow, grey and tall. When they got there she stopped and said: "Right."

He looked at her. Their faces were already submerged in the late afternoon. He saw only a pale oval disc. Then she said: "Yes."

There was a suppressed rattling from her bunch of keys. They laughed.

Then the young man said: "This is the Catharinen-strasse. Thank you."

She sent a look from her colourless jelly eyes through

thick spectacle lenses up to the light blur that must have been his face.

"No," she answered and her eyes appeared somewhat stupid, "I live here. It isn't the Catharinenstrasse. I live here."

The bunch of keys laughed softly.

The young man was taken aback. "Not the Catharinenstrasse?"

"No," she whispered.

"Well, what am I doing here? My God! I really do want to go to the Catharinenstrasse." He spoke very loudly.

Her voice became quite small: "I live here. In this house here." And she rattled her bunch of keys.

Then he understood. He leaned close to the pale oval disc. She's wearing glasses and her eyes are like jelly, so stupid, so limpid, he thought.

"You live here?" he asked and reached for her. "Alone?"

"Yes—of course . . . alone." She paused significantly between each word. Her voice was so new that it frightened even her. In all her thirty-seven years her voice had never been like it was when she said: "I have a room."

He relaxed his hold on her and asked: "And what about the Catharinenstrasse?"

"It's there," she answered and her voice grew again to half of what it had been earlier. "There, second left."

"Second left," he said, and turned round. And through the misty afternoon came the sound of his departing thank you. But it was already far, far away. Then his footsteps died away irresistibly and subsided utterly in the Catharinenstrasse.

No, he did not look back. A grey blur stared at him from behind, but that could have been the house. The house was narrow and tall and grey. That woman, he

5

thought, with her jelly eyes. Just like jelly, they were, so stupid behind her glasses. My God, she must have been at least forty.

And then she said suddenly: I have a room. He grinned at the late afternoon. Then he turned into the Catharinenstrasse.

To the grey, narrow house was stuck a grey blur. It breathed and whispered out loud: "I thought he wanted something. He gave me that look, as if he had no intention of going to the Catharinenstrasse. No, but really he wanted nothing."

Her voice was now back to what it was. As it had been for the past thirty-seven years. Devoid of understanding, her pale eyes swam about behind the thick lenses of her spectacles. As if they were in an aquarium. No, he wanted nothing.

Then she opened the door. And the bunch of keys laughed. Laughed softly. Very softly.

3

THE CHERRIES

⌒∿⌒

In the next room a glass clinked. Now he is eating the cherries which are for me, he thought. It's me who's got the fever. She put the cherries specially outside the window to make them really cold. Now he has smashed the glass. And I have got the fever.

The sick boy got up. He pushed himself along the wall. Then through the door he saw his father sitting on the ground. His whole hand was covered in cherry-juice.

Everything is full of cherries, thought the invalid, everything full of cherries. And I'm the one who's supposed to eat them. I'm the one who's got the fever.

His hand is covered with cherry-juice. They must have been beautifully cold. She put them specially outside the window for my fever. And he's eating all my cherries. Now he's sitting on the floor and his hands are full of them. And I've got the fever. And he's got the cold cherry-juice on his hands. The lovely cold cherry-juice. It was bound to be very cold. It was outside the window specially. For the fever.

He was using the door-handle for support. When it creaked his father looked up.

"Boy, you must go to your bed. With a fever like that, boy. You must go to bed at once."

"Everything is full of cherries," whispered the sick boy. He looked at the hand. "Everything is full of cherries."

"You must go to bed right away, lad." The father tried to get up and grimaced. His hand was dripping.

"All cherries," whispered the invalid, "All my cherries. Were they cold?" he asked out loud. "Yes? They really were nice and cold, weren't they? She put them specially outside the window so that they would be quite cold. So that they would be quite cold."

The father looked up at him helplessly from his position on the floor. He smiled a little. "I can't get up again," he smiled and pulled his face. "It's just too silly for words, but I definitely can't get up."

The invalid was holding on to the door, which moved gently to and fro in time with his swaying. "Were they nice and cold?" he whispered. "Were they?"

"You see, I fell," said the father. "But it's probably just the shock. I'm completely lame," he smiled. "That's because of the shock. It'll be all right in a minute. Then I'll take you back to bed. You must get to bed quickly."

The sick boy was looking at the hand.

"Oh, it's not all that bad. That's only a little cut. That'll soon stop. I got it from the cup," the father dismissed it with a casual wave. He looked up and pulled a face. "I hope she doesn't start cursing. She was very fond of this particular cup. Now I've bust it. It had to be this very cup, the one that she likes so much. I was going to rinse it out when I slipped. I intended to rinse it out with a drop of cold water and put your cherries in it. It's not a bit easy drinking out of a glass in bed. I haven't forgotten that. It's not a bit easy in bed."

The sick boy looked at the hand. "The cherries," he whispered, "what about my cherries?"

Once more his father tried to get up. "I'll fetch them to you at once," he said. "At once, lad. Quick, go back to bed, with your fever. I'll get them for you at once. They're still outside the window, to make them nice and cold. I'll get them for you at once."

The sick boy pushed his way back along the wall to his bed. When his father came with the cherries he had put his head deep under the covers.

4

THE WOOD FOR MORNING

He closed the door of the flat behind him. He closed it gently and without much fuss, although he was about to take his life. The life that he did not understand and in which he was not understood. He was not understood by those whom he loved. And that was the very thing he could not bear, this being at cross purposes with those whom he loved.

But there was something else that became so big that it dominated everything and would not be pushed aside.

This was the fact that at night he could weep without

being heard by those whom he loved. And it was the fact that he saw his mother, whom he loved, growing older, and he saw it happening. And it was the fact that he could sit in a room with the others, laugh with them and yet be lonelier than ever. And it was the fact that the others did not hear the shooting when he heard it; that they never wanted to hear it. This was the being at cross purposes with those whom he loved, which he could not bear. Now he was standing on the landing and was about to go up to the attic and commit suicide. He had spent the whole night thinking about how he would do it and had come to the conclusion that he would have to go up to the attic, for there he would be alone, which was absolutely necessary. He had nothing with which to shoot himself and poisoning seemed to him to be too unreliable. No disgrace would have been worse than to return to life afterwards with the aid of a doctor and to have to endure the reproachful sympathetic faces of the others who were so full of love and anxiety for him. And drowning he found too pathetic; to throw himself out of the window too hysterical. No it would be best to go up to the attic. There one was alone. There it was quiet. There everything was unobtrusive and unfussy. And there above all were the cross beams in the roof-structure. And the linen basket with the washing line. After he had closed the door of the flat quietly behind him he grasped the handrail without further ado and went slowly up the stairs. The conical glass roof over the staircase, reinforced with wire mesh, like spiders' webs, let in the pale light of the sky, which up here near the roof was at its brightest.

Firmly he gripped the clean, light brown handrail and went upstairs without fuss. Then he discovered on the handrail a narrow white streak, which could possibly have been yellow. He stopped and ran his finger over it three or four times. Then he looked back. The white

11

streak went the whole length of the handrail. He bent forward slightly. Yes, one could follow it down into the depths of the darker lower storeys. There it did in any case become a little more brownish, but it nevertheless remained a whole shade lighter than the rest of the wood on the handrail. He let his finger wander a few times along the white streak, then he said suddenly: Fancy! I'd completely forgotten about that!

He sat down on the stairs. Here I was, about to commit suicide and I'd almost forgotten that! I was there when it was done. With the little file which belonged to Karlheinz. I took it in my clenched fist and then I hurtled down the stairs at top speed, all the while keeping the file pressed against the soft wood of the handrail. On the bends I pressed especially hard in order to brake. When I got to the bottom a deep groove ran down the handrail from the attic to the ground floor. That evening all the children were questioned. The two girls amongst us, Karlheinz and me. And the boy next door. The housekeeper said it would cost at least forty marks. But our parents knew at once that it wasn't one of us. A fairly sharp object was involved and none of us had such a thing, they knew full well. Besides, surely no child would deface the handrail in his own house. And all the time it was me. Me with the little pointed file. Since none of the families wanted to pay the forty marks for the repairs the housekeeper added five marks per household to the next rent bill for restoration costs for the seriously damaged staircase. With this money the whole staircase was then laid with linoleum. And Frau Daus got a new pair of gloves to replace those ripped on the splintered handrail. A workman came, planed the edges of the groove smooth and then daubed it with putty. From the attic to the ground floor. And it was me. And now I wanted to commit suicide and had almost forgotten about it.

He sat down on the stairs and took a piece of paper. On it he wrote: I was the one responsible for the handrail. And then above this: to Frau Kaufman, housekeeper. He took all his money out of his pocket, twenty-two marks altogether, and then wrapped the note round it. He stuck it into his top pocket. They're sure to find it there, he thought, they must find it. And he forgot completely that nobody would remember it any more. He forgot that it was now eleven years past, he forgot. He stood up and the stair creaked a little. He now intended to go up to the attic. He had settled the handrail matter and could now go upstairs. There he intended to say again out loud that he could no longer bear being at cross purposes with those whom he loved. Then he would do it.

Downstairs a door opened. He heard his mother saying: And tell her not to forget the soap powder. She mustn't forget the soap powder whatever she does. Tell her that the boy has gone out specially to get the wood so that we can wash tomorrow. Tell her it's a great relief for father, not having to go out with the wood cart and having the boy back again. The boy has gone out specially today. Father says he will enjoy that. He's not been able to do that for all these years. Now he can fetch wood. For us. For tomorrow, for the washing. Tell her that and not to forget my soap powder.

He heard the answering voice of a girl. Then the door was closed and the girl ran downstairs. He could follow her little hand sliding down the handrail to the bottom. Then he could hear only her feet. Then it was quiet. The noise made by the silence could be heard.

He went slowly downstairs, slowly, one step at a time. I must fetch the wood, he said, of course, I'd completely forgotten about that. I really must fetch the wood. For tomorrow.

He went more and more quickly down the stairs, and

13

as he moved he slapped his hand repeatedly on the hand-rail. The wood, he said, I must fetch the wood. For us. For tomorrow. And he jumped down the last few steps in great bounds.

Right at the top the thick glass roof let in the pale light of the sky. Down here, though, the lamps had to be on. All day, every day.

ALL DAIRIES ARE CALLED HINSCH

〰

All dairies are called Hinsch. The Hinsches are blond, and have an air of contentment and well-being like fresh peaches or babes in arms. Hinsches have red, huge hands. Hinsches do not have red hands because they doctor the milk with water. The red hands come from washing the churns and rinsing the bottles. The churns are heavy and the bottles are smooth—that's why the Hinsches' hands are cracked and sore.

Herr Hinsch is big, slow and kind. Frau Hinsch is small and quick, and she is also kind. Elsie, their daughter, is of medium height, lethargic and sullen.

All three Hinsches suffer from cold feet in winter, for the floor is made of flagstones, because they are easier to keep clean. In winter the Hinsches wear black woollen socks inside their clogs—and thick grey scarves round their necks. In winter all three Hinsches have red noses, freezing fingers and chronic colds.

In summer the Hinsches are the only people in our district who do not have to sweat excessively, for the floor is made of flagstones because they are easier to keep clean. In summer the Hinsches find—to their astonishment—that the heat is really quite bearable and they keep their air of peachy freshness. Then they are the envy of all their customers.

Also, because they have more buttermilk then and can close the shop at half-past four because the milk is either all sold or sour. Herr Hinsch is big, good, and fairly morose. Frau Hinsch is small, brisk and friendly. But Elsie is sullen. All the time. Since she was fifteen that's the way she has been. Before that she was like everybody else.

At night the massive long-distance lorries rumble through the hushed streets like overweight artillery and come to a halt outside the dairy, wheezing deep inside and with all sorts of intestinal rattling as if their bronchial tubes were rusted up. They come at night so that people will have milk for their coffee in the morning. The drivers, keepers of these monsters with glowing eyes, are idealists and heroes. They take upon themselves this wearying labour of love and face the unsuspected dangers of the night so that people can have milk in their coffee in the morning.

At the time Elsie was a normal, playful fifteen-year-old, blond and almost too well nourished. The milk trucks used to come at night, and then the three Hinsches used to leave the uneventful paradise of their beds so

16

naturally (even without a sword-bearing angel!); so naturally did they give up the soft warmth of their beds as if there were nothing more natural in the world than to unload nineteen full churns and to load up the trucks with nineteen empty ones in the middle of the night.

Elsie was very blond and very well nourished and she was fifteen years old and it was one of her secret delights to leave her bed, which was overheated by all sorts of strange dreams, and press a few wind-cooled iron churns against her thin dress under the secretive stars. It was like eating ice-cream, bathing or drinking lemonade in summer—only more striking.

The heroic riders of the multi-axled petrol-swilling milk cows, these cowboys of the metropolis, had very soon weighed up the blond wide-hipped girl who so much wanted to be cooled off in the night. My God, in the moonlight all girls look like Madonnas, even the wide-hipped ones.

Heroes, even when they are idealists, heroes who quickly take up position near their trucks in order to relieve themselves of the beer from the last town—indifferent whether or not the wives or daughters of Hinsches happen to be watching (for all dairy-folk are called Hinsch)—these heroes are never prudish. Heroes cannot have the cautiousness of cowards—they must be violent and brutal.

Nevertheless the girl with the wide hips was so shocked and frightened that she let the heavy churn fall onto her head as she was about to stretch both arms up to the truck and suddenly felt a man pressing up against her through her skirts.

The hero had decided that this moment, as she was stretching her bosom so obtrusively upwards but had to embrace the churn with both hands, was the most favourable, and his arms, which were accustomed to

17

leaping about with several hundred horse-power, made a not particularly tender grab. (How could a hero do otherwise!?)

Blond girls, whose bed and blood get too hot in summer, do not always necessarily have a wide-hipped soul. Their soul can be simple and fragile like a child's plaything— and adults can crush it in a second. Girls who get hold of milk churns as gunners handle their shells and experience pleasure in the pressure of the hard metal on their skin, do not necessarily have a big-bosomed soul. Sometimes it happens that they have the sweetest cleanest and most silvery soul in the world—sweet as the scent of flowers, clean as fresh milk and silvery as the fairy wings of many a nocturnal insect.

The hero, lord over an army of horse-powers, lost control of his heart. Of his heart? Yes, maybe even of his heart. He wanted to take Elsie like a bend into which one goes—without slackening speed—he wanted to swing her over like his steering wheel and seize possession of her as he would of a milk churn with his hairy hands.

But the silvery soul, which was as delicate and as easily violated as the shine on a moth's wings was frightened to death in the oily clutches of reality—in a flash the full churn slipped out of the soulless hands and cast an eerie glow on the girl's head; on her blond crown there blossomed thick, dark blood.

That's how it was then, when Elsie after a long illness turned out to be different from what she used to be, different from everybody else. She languished like a primrose which is not given water by the people and which is not granted any sunlight by the window behind which it has to stand.

People said: She is twisted. The Hinsches said: She is sullen. She herself said nothing. Usually she just gave cues to her life, for her silvery soul which was crushed like a moth's wing, was still dreaming about her hero, who perhaps a long time since had sacrificed his brain to the God of Technology on a roadside tree or the pillar of a bridge. Maybe he had let his uncontrolled, love-mad, brimful heart be rolled flat and squeezed dry by the hippopotamus-skinned grey rubber wheels of some strange long-distance lorry, so that he had finished with seeing, hearing and raping in this life.

The next time the ponderous milk trucks brake, trembling, groaning and rumbling, outside the Hinsches' bedroom window then not only the three Hinsches awaken—father Hinsch, mother Hinsch and daughter Hinsch—but also Elsie's restless soul, which begins, roused by the clanging of the milk churns complaining about being forced and banged together onto the pavement, and startled out of its primrose stupor, to make shyly concealed but intoxicating attempts to fly with crushed moth wings. Perhaps she is looking for her hero with the intention of not being so timid as she was last time—but she will not find him. And long after the milk truck has disappeared and the sound of its bells is stilled, she lies awake.

6

THE POST CROWN TOOTH
OR, WHY MY COUSIN
DOESN'T EAT TOFFEES
ANY MORE

It was a nice little cinema. And unpretentious. It reeked of children, excitement, sweets. The whole place reeked of toffee. This was because toffees could be bought in the entrance, near the box-office. Five for two pence. That's why it smelled of toffees from one end to the other. But otherwise it was a nice cinema. And unpretentious. Scarcely two hundred people would fit in it. It was a real suburban little cinema. One of those commonly known as fleapits. Without malice. Our cinema was called the Victoria Picture House. On Sunday afternoons there was a children's show. Half price. But the toffees were almost more important. They were part and parcel of Sunday, of the cinema. Five for two pence. So it was also profitable for the owner.

Unfortunately my cousin had six pence. That meant a multitude of toffees. That made us the happiest amongst the two hundred children. Me too. For I sat next to him and after all he was my cousin. We were very happy. The "unfortunately" did not come until later.

Then, slowly, pleasurably, the lights went down. The lip-smacking sucking noises made by two hundred mouths abated momentarily. Instead the little cinema was drowned by a chorus of Red-Indian howls, the stamping of feet and a prolonged whistling concert. Sunday's blissful announcement of joy, greeting the start of the show.

Then it was dark. The screen grew bright and at the back something whirred. Then there was music. The chorus of Indian howls broke off. In all parts the sucking could be heard again. And the beating of two hundred hearts. The film began.

Afterwards it was impossible to distinguish the details in one's mind. At any rate, there was a great deal of shooting, riding, robbing and kissing. Everything was on the go. Along with two hundred sucking tongues in front of the screen. Later, when called upon to tell all about it, all we remembered was the shooting, riding and robbing. The kissing was suppressed. It was nothing more than rubbish anyway.

The more riding and shooting there was on the screen the more often the toffees were shoved from one cheek to the other. And it could all be heard. A wild chase on horseback appeared on the screen—and the sucking noise swelled like a waterfall.

There was a smell of children, excitement, sweets. And everywhere of toffees.

21

Suddenly, just as the blond, heroically courageous hero was being pursued on his trusty steed by seven black-bearded robbers across the screen-prairie—just as he had cast a penetrating hero's glance at the tragedy-laden sky—just as the criminal pursuers had drawn their deadly accurate six-guns and concealed themselves behind a huge hedge of blooming cacti—there was a scream.

In itself this was nothing extraordinary, for every exciting incident on the screen was sympathetically underlined and commented on by the screams from two hundred children's mouths. But this scream was not in the usual mould. It was too loud and too terrified. It sent a shiver down my spine. Mine particularly, for the one who had screamed was my cousin. And then he screamed again. Loud and lamenting like a puppy whose paw has been trodden on. And then again, a third scream, so hideous in its terribleness that nobody could avoid hearing it. That's how my cousin screamed.

He achieved his objective. Those who were running across the screen stopped in mid-stride, and the whirring came to a halt. The music no longer accompanied the proceedings. The lights went up.

It was not easy to find out from the howling, cursing, sobbing creature that had been my cousin what had provided the stimulus for his three-pronged scream. But then it became clear and the cinema owner who was at the same time cashier and toffee-seller unleashed a coarse oath on his toffees. And, in particular, the toffees he had sold to my cousin.

But of course it was my cousin's fault. It had been drummed into him so often and so urgently, at home and at the dentist's, for Heaven's sake never ever to eat toffees. In spite of all this he had done so. That's when it had happened. The crowned tooth—at that time my cousin had a genuine post crown and we all marvelled at it and revered him—this post crown had been taken in by the toffee and had surreptitiously left its moorings.

And when my cousin had opened his mouth to draw breath during the breathtaking events on the screen, the post crown had insidiously and viciously parted company with its brothers and had rolled away in search of adventure under the cinema seats.

After ten minutes the search had to be abandoned. The post crown had too many advantages on its side. Who would have been so bold as to look for a post crown under the dark seats on which two hundred children were leaping around? Whistling and shouting didn't do any good at all. Perhaps it had long since come to rest in someone's trouser pocket as a piece of pulse-quickening booty. In any case, it was gone.

The lights dimmed again, the screen brightened once more and was set in motion at the point where it had come to a halt. And the music joined in again. And beside me the tear-choked ruins of my recently proudly sucking cousin slumped in melancholy silence.

Everything comes to an end sooner or later. Soonest of all a children's show in a suburban cinema. The screen couldn't take it any longer. Nor the music. They had been strained beyond the limits, so they called a halt. In their place two constantly surprising side doors opened and admitted the bright Sunday afternoon, white and dazzling, into the cinema. In a few minutes the two hundred chattered and prattled out of the doors and out of their Sunday adventure into the Sunday air.

Last of all, with darkened spirits and dark forebodings came my toothless cousin and myself. We looked at each other. Dumb and resigned. And almost manly. Despite our mere twelve years almost manly. To be sure it seemed to me as if there were a terrible warning for me lurking in

23

the eyes of my cousin. This warning said: If you start to laugh now, I shall kill you!

I did not laugh. I did not laugh until five minutes later. But then I laughed all the more heartily.

We were only two or three steps from the exit, and the Sunday sun came flashing towards us, quite inopportunely radiating joy, when there was another scream. This time it was I who screamed.

I stopped dead, as if my toes had been caught in a mousetrap. Then I screamed a second time. With a feeling of imminent triumph.

I've got him!

My cousin could manage no more than the stupid, whispered question: Whom?

Then I screamed for the third time: The post crown! I'm standing on it.

With that I raised my foot from the thick, red, dirty carpet. There was the post crown, lying there as if nothing had happened! The hard little stone that had pressed against my sole was the disloyal tooth. Four hundred feet had probably kicked it through the cinema. It would hardly have ventured so far without assistance.

Now my cousin screamed again, too, to bring the curtain down on the incident.

Then he grabbed the post crown, stared at it reprovingly, but nevertheless happily, and dispatched it—without even at least wiping it on his jacket—back to its proper position.

At last we could laugh. Until the tears ran down our clean Sunday-best collars. For even my cousin would dearly have loved to laugh when the tooth suddenly went missing. If only it hadn't been his tooth. But now it was back in place and we saw no reason why we shouldn't now laugh ourselves silly.

My cousin has never looked at another toffee. Not even looked. I don't blame him.

7

DEAR, BLUE-GREY NIGHT

∽∾

It is not true that night makes everything look grey. It is an indescribable, inimitable blue-grey—grey for the cats and blue for the women—that the night so heavily and so sweetly exhales and that is so intoxicating when it drifts over us, between half-past nine in the evening and a quarter-past four in the morning.

Gentler than the opening of a baby's eyes the blue-grey wafts over us and round us, when our heart is blind and quick of hearing. Our heart is blind and quick of hearing at night and then it hears the night breathing, a flower-blue, mouse-grey breath which will always waft over us and round us, who have a heart that is quick of hearing, wherever we are: Can you smell the strange, soporific blue of night, you in Manhattan and you in Odessa?

Can you smell the sheltering grey that makes the cats in Rotterdam and Frisco sing so sensually, so wistfully?

Can you smell the alcoholic, star-dewy grey-blue of the seductive night, that makes even the most depraved whore in Marseilles into a Madonna when it mingles with her eyelids, in her hair and on her lips?

Can you smell the misty, river-hazy blue-grey that veils our yesterday and hides our tomorrow, can you smell it, you in Altona and you in Bombay? Can you smell the night without being intoxicated by it? Doesn't it intoxicate you?

Tear out your heart, go on, and throw it into the sweet, sensuous lap of the night. Its breath is gentler than the blinking of a maiden and your heart will blossom forth as if under the spell of some incomprehensible charm.

The young who still know nothing, who have only a dark presentiment of everything and are hardly beginning, they are not perturbed. They walk through the streets which are full to overflowing with night—aimless, wordless, timeless.

Perhaps they walk a mere two or three hours side by side, close together, perhaps they walk like this—close, very close—until it starts to get light. Sometimes one of them attempts a small irrelevant word, sometimes the girl answers, afraid of too much closeness. Ah, not of *too* much, but of *so* much closeness. Maybe they come walking again and again down these same streets and over these same desolated, bewitched squares, which are now much more alive because the day takes away their faces. Maybe they have lost their way on the periphery of the city of stone animals, where gardens, lanes and parks are

26

solemnly bedewed and have an air of Sunday desertedness.

They have dreamed themselves on to the periphery of the endless stone desert (alas for the desert!) and now they stand with startled ears and wet shoes: "Oh God, what is that?"

"Frogs."

"Frogs? Do they croak as loud as that?"

"They are singing, Lisa, they are in love. That's why they sing so loud."

"Come off it. Are you really trying to tell me they are singing?"

"Why not? I find it quite pleasant."

"Pleasant, yes— but singing? I think they are laughing. They're laughing at us."

"Why? At us?"

"Because it's been raining for a good few minutes now —and because we're standing out in the middle of it and because we haven't noticed it."

"Summer rain is beneficial. It makes you grow if you don't wear a hat."

"Do you want to grow? I'm sure I'm no taller."

"So that I'll be taller than you, Lisa."

"Must you really be taller than me?"

"I don't know. I just think so."

Let no man come to me and say he doesn't love the rain. Without it the sun would exterminate us all. No, let no man come to me—we all have reason to love it.

Is there any music sweeter than the sound of rain at night? Is there anywhere anything so subtle and so matter of fact, so secretive and so talkative as rain in the night? Are our ears so indifferent that we only react to streetcar bells, cannon blasts or symphony concerts? Do we no longer hear the symphonies of the thousand droplets that prattle and rattle on the pavement by night, that whisper lustfully against windows and roof-tiles, that

27

softly strum and drum fairy tales on the leaves under which the millions of flies have crawled, that drop and plop onto our shoulders through our thin summer clothes or gurgle with tiny gong beats into the stream? Do we no longer hear anything but our own loud ballyhoo?

But the rain also tells stories to half-awake children in the night. For the children he laughs and weeps against the window panes—against their little rosy ears. And he soothes them back into their dreamland.

Is it only the children now who shout with joy as they dance over puddles and overflowing gutters? Is it only the children who laugh at the thick, fat drops that explode on their noses? Are the children the only ones who lie awake, attentive and anxious, as the rain outside blabbers out the most obvious secrets of the world? Is it only children's eyes that the rain makes quiet and big and shining?

Then let us take off the stupid, worn out, inflated dignity of adulthood like a moth-eaten jacket and cast it onto a great heap and burn it up—and let the heavenly rain, the son of the sea and the sun, run through our hair and into our shirts. Let no man come to me and say it isn't worth a cold.

The greengrocer downstairs does not curse even once when the first legion of drops streams in close formation down the cellar steps and splashes him out of his sleep. He digs his wife in her well-covered ribs until she opens her eyes and then both of them, without grumbling, drag the heavy boxes full of vegetables and fruit out of the shop into the narrow back yard. During the long hot day everything had grown withered and sad. Until next morning the night rain would provide a good dousing for the dusty contents of the boxes.

For another few hours the rain slaps against the wall of the house and into the yard with innumerable wet rags—the greengrocer and his wife have long since gone back to sleep. Their broad, rosy cheeks look almost as contented as the old petticoat that the woman had put under the stairs. Comfortable, voluptuous, blissful it lies amidst the legions of slobbering drops which know so many outrageous things about the outside world—the blue woollen petticoat is so inquisitive about the true events of the untrue world that it sucks up the rain until it has lied itself to death. In the morning the stairs will be dry—but the old skirt will be fat and swollen like a great big toad.

And in the doorway of a house:

"I think it's great that we've now got such a good excuse. With all that rain we couldn't possibly get home on time. I think it's splendid don't you?"

"Where you are it's always great. But you're cold— shall I give you my jacket?"

"Of course, then you'll be ill in the morning. Come on, put it over both of us, then we can keep each other warm."

"The frogs are still singing. Can you hear?"

"Don't you think the rain has dampened their ardour yet?"

"Do you really think rain can dampen ardour?"

"Oh, I really don't know what the frogs mean when they sing. Anyway they've got stamina."

"My ardour would not be dampened even by ten cloudbursts. On the contrary!"

"Aha. Whom do you love so deeply, hm?"

"Oh, somebody who is trembling under my jacket, with soaking curls and wet feet."

"Let's not talk about that, not now, all right? It's so dark here and so lonely and we are standing so close together—isn't that enough? Let's be quiet, please. That's much nicer, don't you think?"

"It is raining, it is dark and lonely and we are standing close together—yes, of course, it's beautiful. . . ."

After twenty-seven minutes:

"Don't you think the rain is an angel? My mother would have played merry hell if she had noticed that I had used make-up. Just seventeen and dolling yourself up like a—like one of those, you know, that's what my mother says. Now the rain has licked it all off and I don't need to mess up my handkerchief. Isn't the rain an angel? . . ."

After eleven minutes:

"Do you want to go home, Lisa?"

"No—Do you?"

"Heavens, if anybody had heard that: Neither of us wants to go home any more! Yes, the rain is an angel."

8

THE THUNDERSTORM

The sky was green. And there was a scent of fear. The evening smelled of beer and fried potatoes. The narrow, endless streets smelled of people, potted plants and open bedroom windows.

The sky turned a poisonous yellow. The world was hushed with anxiety. Only a giant bus snorted past, primeval and asthmatic. It left a trace of oil fumes in the air.

The Alster river turned pale and stared like a fearful animal's eye through the mass of houses to the sky. It saw the inevitable approaching. And it became so pale that it looked as if a hundred thousand fishes had suddenly turned their bellies upwards. The church steeples were near and seemed naked. The city cringed.

On the wall of a house two snails moved slimily past without greeting each other, in solitary calmness. For six hours they had stuck there, facing each other, each expecting the other to move out of the way. Then at last they made a joint decision and set off at the same time. And each left a thin, slippery silver trail on the wall.

From the multi-storey house there was hardly a sound. A door miaowed. And a child asked something. Nothing else. Only downstairs in the entrance two hearts were beating. They belonged to a young man and a girl.

When the two snails, watched by the two people, had moved a hand's breadth away from each other a window grated loudly and unmistakably shut. A surprising wind started whining, picked up a scrap of paper, clattered an empty jam jar against the cobblestones and howled through the paralysed city like a hundred hungry dogs. Gigantic drops of rain splashed coldly and rhythmically onto the streets.

When the first flash went across the sky like a rip the girl reached for the hand of the young man and pressed it to her breast. The thunder barked petulantly above the roof tops. For seconds both closed their eyes.

The young man was a typical man. He wanted not only to keep the position which he had won so easily but counted the thunderstorm as an unashamed stroke of luck for himself. And he put his other hand alongside and drew the girl to him entirely.

The girl looked at him as if she were seeing him for the first time. He nodded at her grandly: Yes, now I've done it. But then she took his hands away from her, quickly and silently. And because she understood him she was breathing excitedly: "Oh you. I don't understand what you're doing." Then she ran out into the rain.

The young man was a typical young man. He saw the improbably fat wet raindrops and shrugged his shoulders: No, I don't understand it either. Shaking his head he picked up one of the snails and put it back where it had been an hour earlier. He wiped his hand on his trousers and sat down dejectedly on the stairs. He chewed grimly on a rubber band.

Gradually the flashes faded. The thunderbolts smothered their rage. The Alster chatted gurglingly with the fat raindrops. There was a fertile scent of milk and earth. The bark of the trees was a bluish grey and gleamed like the hide of an elephant just emerging from the river. In a side street nearby a car hissed through the puddles.

The young man weighed up the sky. Up there hung a thin moon. The sky was transparent and clean like a freshly polished window pane. The air was silky and the first stars were embroidering a wavering pattern in the approaching night. People could be heard breathing deeply in sleep. But the trees, the flowers and the grass were awake, drinking. The last thunder made as little noise as a child moving a chair.

9

THE WALL

⁓⁕⁓

In the end only the wind will remain. When everything else is gone, tears, hunger, machines and music, then there will only be the wind left. He will outlive everything, stone and street, even immortal love. And he will sing comfortingly in the sparse shrubs which crown our snow-clad graves. And on summer evenings he will court the sweet flowers and playfully dance with them—today, tomorrow, always.

He is the first and last great symphony of life and his breath is the eternal melody singing over cradle and coffin. And beside his whispering, roaring lispings, thundering and whistling nothing else will exist. Not even Death, for the wind sings over the crosses and the bones and where he sings there is Life. For the flowers belong to him and they laugh at bony old Death, the flowers and the wind.

Wise is the wind for he is as old as Life.

Wise is the wind, and he can blow mightily and meekly, just as he wishes.

His breath is power and there is nothing that can stand in his way.

Once there was an isolated, battered old wall which had formerly belonged to a house. She now stood there unsteadily searching with hollow eyes for the meaning of her existence. And she reared up into the sky, threatening, humble, deserted.

When the evening wind took her in his tender arms she swayed gently and sighed. His embrace was warm and soft, for the wall had grown old and fragile and sorrowful. His embrace comforted her, it was so soft, and she sighed once more.

"What is the matter?" asked the young wind tenderly.

"I am lonely. I am meaningless. I am dead," sighed the old wall.

"Ah, you are sad because they have forgotten you. You have protected them for a lifetime, their cradles, their weddings, their funerals. But they have forgotten you. Leave them, the world is ungrateful," the young wind knew, because he was so wise.

"Yes they have forgotten me. I have lost my meaning. Oh, they are ungrateful, the people," moaned the old wall.

"Finish it!" urged the wind.

"How?" asked the wall.

"Avenge yourself," whispered the wind.

"How can I?" she wanted to know.

35

"Collapse," he murmured voluptuously.

"Why?" she trembled.

Then the young wind swirled round in front of the old wall, so that her stiff bones crackled and she saw way down at her feet the people hurrying by, the ungrateful people. And a quiver ran through the whole frame of the old, deserted wall as she saw the people again and asked the wind: "Can—I—really—collapse?"

"Do you want to? Then you can"—came the oracular reply from the wordly-wise wind.

"I will try it," sighed the wall. "Yes!"

"Then collapse!" shrieked the wind and crushed her in his young arms and bent her and pressed himself close up to her and heaved up a little and cracked her. Then he let her go and her resistance was at an end.

She was now bending right over. Far below her thronged the ungrateful forgetful, faithless little people to whom she had remained true all her life. And when she saw the little people scurrying down there, so tiny, she forgot her hate and her vengeance. For really she loved people, swarming and minute. And then she was sorry and now at the very last moment she wanted to be upright again.

But the wind was on his guard against such an idea. And he gave the old, fragile wall a kick, so that she hurtled down in a crashing creaking mass onto the street below.

She killed an elderly woman and two children and a young man just on his way home from the war. She screamed, that dying, smashed old wall and with her last croaking breath she asked the young wind:

"Why? Why did you do that? I loved them!"

But the wind laughed as the wall met her end. He had energy to spare and was ancient and wise. He laughed at Life for he knew that that was how it had to be. And he had no heart, the ancient young wind.

But he could be soft when the mood took him. And so, as the old wall died, sobbing because she had killed four people, he sang her to sleep, eternal sleep.

But then the young wind laughed again, for he outlives everything: stone and street and even immortal love.

10

TUI HOO

As a small, bursting buckskin sausage travelled rhythmically back and forth over the bright red varnished fingernails, the page of a calendar pushed itself in front of Ludovico's watery fish eyes: 25th April.—25th April? Ludovico performed an exaggerated asthmatic sigh and his shoulders slumped. 25th April? No idea. In a mildly excited but unimaginably dull-witted fashion the buckskin sausage polished these spade-shaped fingernails, which might have been digging in all sorts of rubbish. It, too, knew nothing about the 25th April.

Suddenly it stopped in mid-sweep, as if listening to the

clock, which was starting to wheeze and chuckle. Not quite still, for Ludovico's big feeble hand was still trembling slightly from its exertions of polishing. Well, at sixty-seven years of age one no longer had the strength of a youth, even if one otherwise—and from the mirror in the corner came an assenting nod—still looked quite passable. To be chief cook on the big ocean-going luxury liners was a spiritual and artistic profession which did not develop muscles on one's arms. As an apprentice, swishing about with giant spoons in giant soup pans one soon packed fine muscles onto one's arms, but, heavens, that was a good half-century ago. Now the packing was round the waistline but this was compensated by the fact that one's sense of smell and taste had been refined to such an extent that they had a claim to a certain artistic fame.

The leather sausage hovered so long over the left hand until the shell-adorned clock had grown calm after its nine coughing strokes. Then once more Ludovico's carp-lips breathed delicately on the excessively long thumb-nail and the buckskin pressed the last lingering dullness to a rosy high polish. Two thin arms and two thin legs heaved the two-hundredweight rotundity out of the basket chair; leather sausage, polishing stone and nail-file somersaulted into a box and Ludovico launched himself in the direction of the mirror, then after briefly checking his hairdo he contently saluted his reflection. There we are then, Ludovico!

Before an Italian duke in a fit of alcoholic high spirits had bawled across the dining room: Ahoy, you old barrel, another two pounds of caviar! Ludovico—Ludovico! Another two pounds of caviar, d'you hear?—until then Ludovico had been called, plain and simple, Ludwig Marusche, born in Hamburg, Altona, and occasionally had his little finger in the proximity of his nostrils. Meanwhile Ludovico had snuggled into a pilot-cloth coat, rammed a distinguished bowler hat onto the back of his head and was now standing downstairs at the front door. Indeed, at sixty-seven he was hardly full of the joys of youth, but he was still in quite good trim and his cooking at sea had enabled him to build a tidy nest-egg. Now he was the quiet, well-dressed boss of a big night-club, slept until lunchtime and spent his evenings keeping an eye on things, waving a greeting to the regulars and whispering to the thoroughly decent girls a few not so thoroughly decent compliments. That was something a sixty-seven-year-old could do quite well, particularly since the goldmine by the name of "Red Christine" was in the sweet and efficient hands of Lotti and Irma, whom he had picked up somewhere or other and who now clung to him as if they were his own daughters.

The moon, the old pale lemon, sailed silently and longingly around the slender body of St. Catharine, whose verdigrised hair loomed over the mosaic carpet of dark red roofs like a somnolent seagull cry. The mist ghosted in patched underpants from the harbour through the empty streets, and lazily came to rest, hanging on a lonely lamp-post. From time to time a cat howled—or a woman. Sometimes there were footsteps, growing louder as they approached from somewhere and died away in some other direction. It really is a bit quiet, thought Ludovico and speedily jerked his legs out of the folds of his paunch as if a mad dog was thinking of having a go at his trousers from behind. His heels clattered in a feeble and anxious rhythm against the endless walls of the houses, in which only now and then the monotony was broken by a green or red lampshade.

There was a rumbling. Down in the harbour. A rumbling and a grumbling, a howling and a yowling, a wailing

40

and a hailing. And it was sounding slowly nearer. Nearer and nearer and louder and louder. Ludovico stopped and stood like a statue. Without moving, without thinking, without breathing. Just his ears were growing, growing to a grotesque size, growing into gigantic funnels, which didn't miss the slightest sound or stir. And all at once he realised that the music was familiar. His hands fluttered up to his neck, but he couldn't raise a scream for just then Tui Hoo swished round the corner, clapped his mouth shut with a resounding slap, and thrust his cry of terror back down his throat.

Tui Hoo has no respect for statues. At least, not just because they were corpulent and had red-varnished nails —no, Tui Hoo was no bourgeois who got worked up about his neighbour because he was wearing a funny hat. He played around with women who smoked cigars and who were as hoarse as watering cans, or with men who wore earrings and whose trouser-legs were wide, like women's dresses. No, Tui Hoo was not petty. But statues whose hearts conked out because they were scared stiff, statues who were cowardly and who lived to be sixty-seven because others of fifteen had to believe in them— Tui Hoo hated statues like that and leapt spitting at them like an overwrought, starved, wildcat, like—in fact like a regular rebellious gale who was good and cruel like his mother the sea and who by rights was at home amongst herring-boats and wood freighters, who conversed with monosyllabic sailors between top-mast and jib-boom. But sometimes he rushed off course upstream into the port and then he rammed and rattled the hearts and windows of the well-to-do, as if he wanted to subject even them to his might. And whenever Tui Hoo went on shore then he always bought himself a good old acquaintance who had got away from him at sea, and who at sea had been a louse. Those were the ones he

41

bought himself. Tui Hoo, old and blown to bits, the green-blue child who played with the fishes, Tui Hoo, the mad fluter, the great organist, the heavenly musician. Tui Hoo, the breath of the world.

"Do you remember him, Ludwig Marusche? Eh, Marusche, don't you know Tui Hoo any more? Tui Hoo, hoo, do you remember, Ludwig, when you were cook on the 'Black Karin' twenty years ago? Have you forgotten it all, harmless old gentleman, eh? Forgotten it all, have you?"

With his neck bent Ludovico fought his way through the silent streets, in which Tui Hoo was grinding away on his hurdy gurdy. But Tui Hoo, the sea wind, was no boring toothless barrel-organ grinder, not in vain had he washed with the waters of all the seas: hupp—he took the old man unexpectedly from behind, played with the terror-stricken two-hundredweight ball, grabbed with a thousand fingers the waved top knot, pointed it steeply up to the sky for a moment which lasted as long as breath, then he whirled the stiff pomaded locks into such a tangle that the vain old fellow's cold sweat of fear trickled into his eyebrows.

At an insane speed Tui Hoo chased his victim over perilously bumpy pavements, blew out in passing the lamps that were dim in any case and then suddenly, as if he had forgotten him, he took the wind out of his sails, so that Ludovico's coat lost its extravagant, shapeless inflation and reeled down about him like a piece of potato peel. Tui Hoo simply let him stand there in the pitch-dark night. But soon he picked up his baton to conduct the next movement of the mad concert. It assaulted the dead tired Ludovico's face at the next corner, with a tui and a hoo, so that he had to pit the whole of his two hundredweight against it to avoid being tipped out of his patent leather shoes.

"Hoo, hoo, Marusche, you old rogue, have I shifted all the dust and fear and whitewash out of the twists of your brain? Would you kindly remember, eh? Do you recall? Oh, you remember! Twenty years ago on the 'Black Karin' when the seamen called me Tui Hoo. Don't you think about the night of 25th April any more, you cowardly old rascal, hoo?"

Yes, that was Tui Hoo, friend of the stout-hearted, enemy of cowards. That was Tui Hoo, who pressed the girls' skirts against their knees and scared off the flies from the cradles of babes in swaddling clothes. That was Tui Hoo who came upon his enemies as strangler and destroyer, as ghost, as murderer and killer. That was Tui Hoo!!! And now he huffed and puffed this broken, rigged-up, corpulent bar-owner through the lonely starless night, through a night without pity.

Then scraps of paper fluttered up high out of the gutter—newspapers, sandwich papers, torn-up love letters; endless calendar pages—25th April—25th April—Tui Hoo clenched his fist and drew it back for an unavoidable blow that wouldn't miss its target. And he screamed at the cook of the "Black Karin": "Think back to the 25th April, you dog!" And then Tui Hoo attacked with all his might, tore off roofs, hurled three-masters as high as the houses and threw the cook Ludovico Marusche of the "Karin" head over heels down the cellar stairs of his own night club, thudding his brain box, which was paralysed with fear, against the door.

The "Red Christine" was a reputable night-club—and when something suddenly thundered against the door with all its might then that was regarded as a sensation in the "Red Christine". It was a few seconds before Irma realised that this old man covered in filth was her boss, her darling good little boy. The people in the alcoves and sitting on the barstools filed with curious horror

43

around the reclining figure, who seemed to have made himself comfortable in such a comically crumpled pose outside his own door. But they had to leave him lying like that on the cellar steps, for even the slightest movement brought blood trickling from his twisted mouth.

Helpless, scared and embarrassed, insolent or indifferent, the heroes of night-life stood around the dying old man. Irma, pompous and voluptuous like a Wagner-singer, raised his peculiarly bent head from the cold stone steps and nestled it into her warm soft lap. As if she were nursing a God just returned exhausted by good works, raven-haired Lotti was cleaning and cooling the disfigured face of her good old grandpa, but she could not manage to wipe the naked, delirious fear out of his wrinkles, even if her handkerchief *had* been dipped in champagne. Lotti, gentle as a gazelle, was kneeling beside the motionless fleshy giant, trying to find his pulse under the broad gold bracelet of his watch. And the stupid, apathetic phantom-like creatures of the night who surrounded the two hostesses, silent and pale, did not know whether the look on Lotti's face registered fright or joy at the feeble heartbeat—and they didn't know whether Irma's tiny plump hands were fingering Ludovico's collar out of pity or an urge to strangle him.

Tui Hoo, triumphantly squatting on the top step of the cellar staircase, was waiting for death and he knew that he did not have long to wait. Nimbly he got up, wriggled his way through the circle of revellers, making them start to shiver, imperceptibly, and sat down with his knees drawn up, on Irma's round, rather plump thigh, in such a position that he was able, without undue exertion and in the greatest possible comfort, to whisper one more ever so tiny story into old Ludovico's ear.

"No, Ludwig Marusche, you are not going to miss a single word of the story of the 25th April, of the 'Black

44

Karin', and of Tui Hoo. I, Tui Hoo, the ancient young God of the winds that blow across the world's seas, am perched here on the worn-out cellar steps of a shady night club to wheeze this story once again in every detail into your ears, you old dog, so that you will be well prepared for your long, long journey to Hell."

Ludwig Marusche raised his arched, creased eyelids. A fear flickered in his pupils that was so terrible that no scream could possibly relieve it. "Have you forgotten, you old rogue? Yes, it was then when I found you, late in the evening of the 25th April in the Kattegatt and drove you before me for a few hours with a tui and a hoo! It was bitterly cold and I was ready for my best tricks when I saw your nutshell amongst the mammoth waves. The crew were as tired as flies and the Old Man had not left the bridge day or night. But of course you didn't notice any of that, for in your galley it was warm and so sheltered that you would have noticed the draught made by a cockroach going round the coffee pot.

"Then a shipmate came dashing through your door to where your pots and pans were. The Old Man wanted a mug of hot tea. But you were supposed to take it to him yourself so that your fifteen-year-old galley boy wouldn't be swept off the deck by the wind. And I was the wind, Marusche, have you forgotten? What a coward you were, fatty! Ten steps you took with that tea, then you couldn't bear my gentle song in your drooping flabby ears any longer. What a pitiful fright sat on your piggy fat neck and then caught you unawares as it rushed down into your belly when I did a somersault between your legs. Shame on you, soup king, you never ever embraced a harbour girl as passionately as you did the mast which on that night of the 25th April stood in your path like a helpful angel. For a moment you hung at the mast like an empty suit, but then you were seized with the courage

45

of a general and in four mighty bounds you reached the salvation of your galley. And Heini Hagemann, your little galley boy, suddenly had the tea thrust into his hands and was sent by you out into the misty night to the Old Man. The Old Man never got his tea. Heini never reached the bridge. The tea mug was found somewhere next morning. Heini Hagemann wasn't. He wasn't found next morning. Nor that evening. Nor on the day after that. Because a grown man was a coward! You are an ungrateful swine if you could forget that the only reason you lived to be sixty-seven years old, was that little Heini Hagemann went instead of you. But never mind, Marusche, in a few seconds you will meet your kitchen boy. Don't goggle so fearfully, old chap. Even Heini Hagemann pulled himself together when he went overboard. The little fellow was quite calm."

A milky haze covered the wide open eyes of Marusche. Maybe it *was* a slight, mean smile that stole furtively across Lotti's blood red mouth. And then his fish-mouth lips released the last breath: tui——hoo——.

Arrogantly Tui Hoo tore a lock from Irma's artful blond hairdo and left it swinging to and fro on her forehead. Then he rose up singing and whistling through the wall of sympathetic gapers—hui too hui—and howled downstream to the open sea.

STRANGE

I

Strange, thought Sixth Former Hans Hellkopf during the war, the commander of our battalion always reminds me of my teacher.

II

Strange, thought Sixth Former Hans Hellkopf after the war, our teacher always reminds me of the commander of my battalion. It must be his hairstyle.

47

III

Strange, said the teacher Dr. Olaf to his colleague; when I see our Sixth Formers filing in from the school yard it always makes me think of my battalion. It must be their fresh shining faces. Their faces? said his colleague. Their boots, old man, their boots.

12

PRUSSIA'S GLORY

∽✠∾

The naked skull swam like a highly polished moon under the pale nightlights. It swam through the dead factory. And the nightlights twinkled down like pale stars. Under the naked skull marched a gaunt, erect man. He threw his long legs high in front of him. His footsteps exploded against the high, cold walls and fell resoundingly from the ceiling back to the floor. It echoed as if a battalion were marching. But it was only a gaunt, erect man with long legs and a bald head marching in the lonely factory. Marching with a bald head that swam through the nocturnal half-light of the factory like a brass moon, jerkily, pale and highly polished.

The long legs pushed alternately straight out in front. The gaunt man was marching an exemplary, faultless parade-step through the gigantic bare rectangle of the factory hall. Forwards went the legs. They were jabbed high into the air by the gaunt man. They were marching an exemplary, faultless parade-step, those long legs which belonged to the bald head. And from the skull which gleamed like brass beneath the pale nightlights a tinny voice grated out the marching song of Prussia's fame and honour, Prussia's Glory: Dadadam . . .Dadamdadamda-dam . . .

But then the tin music stopped suddenly. A rather effeminate tenor gave a command from the skull, burst onto the silence like a gunshot; the night was torn apart in fright at this shout: Battaliooon—Halt! The gaunt man stood motionless as a rod in the hall. Then it came again from the skull, tenor, tenor, gunshot and tin: Leeeeefft—turn! The gaunt man threw his right leg far away from himself and turned his body on his left heel with the speed of lightning. His dusty grey eyes stared lifelessly at the high wall of the factory. In the wall there was a window and outside was the night, looking in at the gaunt erect rod in the hall. Then again from the bare skull came the gunshot in the lonely hall, effeminate tin-cry in the silent night: Presennt—arms! The gaunt man's arms, which until this moment had stuck stiff and lifeless to his body, were jerked upwards and waited at an angle across his chest. There was not a sound in the benighted hall. But then the tenor grated out of the skull again, tinnily, tinnily he grated the marching song of Prussia's fame and honour, Prussia's Glory: Dadadamdamdadam . . .

Bewildered, the remains of the startled night crept away into the corners of the lonely hall. And only two old red-eyed rats filed past the gaunt erect man, squeaking softly—Prussia's Glory. Red-eyed rats in the dead hall.

Tin music from a bare skull. Prussia's Glory: Dadadam-dadadamdam . . .

But outside the window two faces broadened into a malicious grin. Two dark figures dug their elbows into each other's ribs. Then the grinning faces slipped away from the window and the darkness swallowed them up. Right at the end of the street they could still hear the faint sound of the solitary tenor from the hall behind them: Dadadamdadamdadam . . .

The next morning the gaunt erect man stood in an office. There was a desk, a filing cabinet and a soiled towel. And over the desk hovered a sleepy face. It was completely covered in sleep and only the mouth was to some extent awake. And it was so sluggish that the lower lip hung down tiredly. The sleepy face had a voice like velvet, so soft and so pleasantly gentle. And the voice drifted yawningly over to the gaunt man who stood before the desk. He stood very erect before the desk and his dusty grey eyes looked through the sleepy face at the soiled towel. And he became a little more erect when the drifting soft velvet voice reached him!

"You are the nightwatchman?"

"Yes."

"Since when?"

"The end of the war."

"And before that?"

"Soldier."

"What?"

"Colonel."

"Thank you."

The gaunt man stood like a rod before the desk, motionless, stiff, indifferent. Only his grey eyes looked the towel up and down. Then from the desk came drifting the velvet soft drowsy voice again:

51

"Last night somebody broke in. In the factory. You were asleep."

The rod remained silent.

"Well?" drifted the voice.

The rod remained silent.

The sleepy face shook disapprovingly from left to right.

"As you wish. Tomorrow there will be an investigation. You will have to appear as a witness. Tricky business, sir. Did you have a hand in it?"

The tired face smiled sweetly. The rod stood very erect and said nothing.

The velvet voice yawned: "Well, as you wish. You'll have to talk tomorrow. Either you were asleep. Or you were involved in it. Let's hope they believe you. Thank you, you can go."

Then the gaunt man turned round and marched to the door. From there he grated back at the sleepy face and held his gleaming skull somewhat on one side: "Is the investigation in public?"

Then the velvet voice became quite delicate and whispered: "Yes. In public, sir. In public."

"In public," repeated the gaunt man and the skull nodded too. "Right then, in public."

"In public," yawned the sleepy one again.

Then the gaunt man opened the door and closed it again. Inside, the soiled towel swung gently to and fro in the draught caused by the door.

"In public," said the man and held a gleaming piece of metal in his hand. Twice, three times he let it click. He saw two grinning faces. He saw a courtroom which was packed with people. And both the faces were grinning. And then the whole courtroom grinned.

"Prussia's Glory," he said softly. "Prussia's Glory. And the whole city is present."

The metal in his hand clicked. Then the hand raised the metal up to the gleaming skull.

Soon afterwards a gaunt, erect man lay quiet on the floor like a broken rod. Beside him lay the piece of metal. And the naked skull lay like an extinguished moon in the half-darkness of the room. Like an extinguished moon. And over him marched an endless battalion to the sounds of Prussia's Glory. A glorious marchpast. Marching past: Dadadamdadamdadam . . .

Or was it the rain? The rain on the dark red tiles? For it was raining. Raining incessantly.

13

SUNDAY MORNING

The morning service on the radio had come to its conclusion amidst the drone of organ music. Amen. Dear
old God was still as efficient as ever. Hallelujah. Sergeant
Soboda's short-fingered rectangular hand turned the radio
louder. They were playing martial music. He loved martial
music. Then he took his sweaty, leather, stinking service
cap from the table, bubbled another Amen and jammed
it back onto his head, which looked as if it had been
polished. The hard rim of the cap buried itself in the
furrowed groove which was the result of decades of
wearing this cap on his bald head in the regulation

54

manner. The rim of the cap had to settle into this furrow then everything was in order: The cap sat accurately two fingers' breadth above the ears. This had been ordained by the experts generations ago in the service regulations. The constantly reddened furrow which encircled the billiard ball was the symbol of soldierly obedience. With the reddened furrow two fingers' breadth above the ears an ancient tradition was being honoured and maintained, even if Nature had still not gone over to producing custom-built heads for service caps. Amen, then—the cap was in place.

Then he opened his pocket-knife. It was a fine knife even if it did only have one blade. But it was a good blade. A fine knife. Properly speaking, it was crude, ordinary and brutal. But in his opinion it was a fine knife. So it was. One was able simply and without exception to do everything with it. Everything: graft fruit trees, scrape out briar pipes, slice bread, dismantle watches, clean one's fingernails, sharpen pencils, carve artificial honey. It was a splendid knife. And it had the inscrutable magic smell of an oriental fairy tale: wood, tobacco, bread, watch oil and honey.

This morning was Sunday, and three aromas, the three typical Sunday morning aromas wafted, around the somewhat tired, but still conscientious blade: the smell of tobacco from cleaning the pipe before the service—the smell of soil, allotment garden soil from the regular Sunday cleaning of the fingernails during the service—and thirdly the smell of artificial honey from carving a rock-hard block of honey after the service. And this carving of honey was the most important Sunday morning ceremony, and that was why the knife had been opened.

After a small, sticky cube of artificial honey was stowed away behind the nicotine stained stumps which

55

were all that remained of his teeth, he shoved his stool back with a powerful shuffling movement, for he never got up any other way, and with the aid of his rectangular hands which he supported on the grease-spotted, ink-stained table, he got to his feet. Then he reached for a black varnished leather belt, on the inside of which two words had been crudely daubed with copying ink in big, legible letters: Sergeant Soboda. The dice of artificial honey changed over from the left to the right cheek, then Sergeant Soboda raised his left leg, according to the regulations, and began his tour of duty: Second inspection of cells One to Twenty. Sunday morning. Eight-forty.

As the hobnailed and yet soulful footsteps (which could be those of a bandy-legged old porter) became audible at the end of the Sunday-quiet, peacefully dusty corridor, all the prisoners who were in Sergeant Soboda's section pressed their faces into expectant Sunday creases and their ears to the doors of their cells. With relish they awaited the usual Sunday conversation with Number Nine. Amongst the inmates of these thick, dense walls only three did not take part in this ritual: Number One, Number Seventeen and Number Nine.

Number One had no time. He was a lifer and in twenty-three years he had achieved the position of toady. That is, he emptied the lavatory buckets and filled the food tins, and on Sunday mornings he had no time. On this day he regularly got a huge bundle of old newspapers in his cell. Swiftly he read the speeches of the great statesmen, then he tore them up (the speeches) into sheets roughly the size of the palm of a hand. That was his job. These sheets were passed through the trapdoor when food was being issued at lunchtime. Every cell got thirty-four sheets. To last until the next Sunday. Toilet paper. (Swiftly, the torn up speeches of the great statesmen were read and then used—the speeches). This was a cultured community.

Nor did Number Seventeen put his ear to the door of the cell in order to participate in the Sunday conversation. For he was weeping. He was sixteen years old and he wept. It was Sunday and he was in prison and he had stolen a bicycle. He wept tearlessly, comfortlessly, noiselessly. The whole quite pitiful sorrow of human history rode on shrilly jingling bicycles across the scribbled walls of his cell: bicycles—bicycles—for hours on end bicycles, bells tinkling. He was weeping because it was Sunday at home and they were having sponge cake and thinking of him. They were thinking of him, by God they were, but they were also having sponge cake. That was why Number Seventeen was weeping on Sunday morning at eight-forty and was not holding his ear to the door of his cell.

And Number Nine? Number Nine couldn't hold his ear to the door of his cell because he had his mouth there. He had his mouth there every Sunday morning. This was the time he had to speak to section leader Sergeant Soboda about an urgent matter. And Sergeant Soboda could not hear very well. Therefore Number Nine had to keep his mouth right up against the door of his cell.

And then—as the hobnailed footsteps thundered soulfully towards them, all the prisoners in Sergeant Soboda's section underwent with shaking of heads or giggling their Sunday experience. All except Number One who was tearing up political speeches for toilet paper. And Number Seventeen, who was weeping.

"What's the matter, Number Nine?"

"Permission to speak to you, Sergeant."

"Yes, go on."

"Permission to ask if I can take possession of my toothbrush."

"Where is it Number Nine?"

"With my belongings."

"No."

"But it is, Sergeant."

"Yes, it may well be there. But you are not getting it."

"Could it not be arranged that my toothbrush be handed to me, as an exception to the rules?"

"No."

"And—why not, Sergeant?"

"Because prisoners are not allowed access to their belongings."

"Why are they not allowed access, Sergeant?"

"It is forbidden."

"And couldn't you perhaps, Serge . . .?"

"No."

"And why not, Ser . . .?"

"Because officers are not allowed access to prisoners' belongings."

"But why not, if I—"

"It is forbidden."

"Why is that forbidden, then?"

"Because it has always been forbidden."

"Couldn't there possibly be any exception, Serge . . .?"

"No."

"Why not, Ser . . .?"

"Because it is forbidden, I tell you!"

"Not even just this once—after all it's only a matter of a toothbrush!"

"No."

"Why not, Ser . . .?"

"Because we've never allowed it before."

"But why is it not possible?"

"Because prisoners are not allowed access to their belongings."

"Would it not perhaps be possible for you, Serg . . .?"

"No."

"And why—well, why not?"

"Because officers are not allowed access to prisoners' belongings."

"Sergeant, permission to ask a question."

"Go on, yes!"

"What is the best way to conduct myself?"

"How do you mean?"

"Well, if I want to have my toothbrush?"

"Oh, I see. If that's what you want. Well, write an application."

"Do you think I could possibly have some paper today? And ink, Ser . . ."

"No."

"Why not, Ser . . .?"

"Because you are only allowed to write every eight weeks and it's only four weeks since you wrote."

"But surely I could write to my lawyer!"

"That makes no difference!"

"Is there nothing at all . . .?"

"No."

"But I just can't sit here for months on end without a toothbrush!"

"Think yourself lucky you've still got your head on your shoulders. You'll manage to survive your last four years."

"But that's dreadful. I can't last forty-eight months without a toothbrush!"

"Oh, you can't, eh? Let me tell you something. I'm fifty-seven years old and I've never touched one of those things in my life. The whole village I come from doesn't play around with such things. And they've all grown old. Even without a toothbrush. Understand? What I can do, you can do too, understand? You're not having it, understand! Understand?"

"Yes, Ser . . ."

"Right, then."

"Yes, sir."

Kindly, conscientiously, his mind filled with Sunday thoughts and with peace in his heart, Sergeant Soboda ended his second tour of inspection of cells One to Twenty. Sunday morning. Ten-past nine.

All the prisoners in Sergeant Soboda's section took their ears from the doors of their cells and giggled or shook their heads. And kicked the wall because they were so amused or so angry.

All except Number One. And Number Seventeen. And Number Nine.

Number Nine slumped onto his stool, exhausted by his battle against the might of the State, and vented his impotent hatred on his wooden clogs. That's what he did every Sunday. The rest of his mind was filled with thoughts of the pink tinge of his toothbrush. It was pink and had cost two marks forty-five. And he would never see it again.

Number One was not giggling either. Nor was he shaking his head. He was tearing toilet paper. Thirty-four sheets for each cell. Afterwards, lunch time. He was a lifer and in twenty-three years he had reached the position of toady.

He emptied the lavatory buckets and filled the food tins. On Sunday mornings he tore up the speeches of the great statesmen into toilet paper. He had committed no crime. If anybody asked him, he used to say: I just happened to be there. No, he was innocent. And therefore he tore up toilet paper contentedly and patiently. Every Sunday. Thirty-four sheets, until lunch time. All his life.

And Number Seventeen was still weeping. He was sixteen years old and it was Sunday and at home they were thinking of him and eating cake. They were thinking of him—but they were still eating cake. And they had no idea what those tinkling bicycles were like that rode through his brain for hours on end.

They were eating cake and he was sitting here weeping.

It was Sunday morning.

14

CHING LING, THE FLY

I suppose you think that's much too nice a name for a fly? Well, in that case I'd better tell you how the fly Ching Ling came to get such a peculiar name. Then you'll have to admit that at least it's an original name. Please listen.

Have you ever sat in a prison cell? Pardon me, of course you haven't! But I can assure you it isn't very hard to get in. The reverse, that is, getting out, is generally much harder to achieve. As I learned at my trial I was supposed to have made somewhere, at some time, in a condition not dissimilar to that produced by alcoholic intoxication, a derogatory remark about somebody. One should never do that. Hamlet also found that out because he considered that something was rotten in the State of Denmark.

Hamlet, too, was not allowed to say so, when he—anyway, it makes no difference now. The important thing at the moment is that you learn why I called the fly Ching Ling.

I was sitting in a state of total collapse under the annihilating accusations of the court, shrouded in impenetrable clouds of spiritual gloom, with an empty stomach and my knees pulled up under my chin in my cell, staring with almost fakir-like composure at one of the unadorned walls when suddenly, right in front of my darkened eyes a small, perfectly ordinary household fly was sitting on the wall. Or rather, she was standing, for flies cannot sit down at all. She appeared so suddenly, like an ink blotch in a mathematics exercise book.

In a flash I remembered the days of old, into which the days of my childhood room must once have fallen, and I asked her politely how I could be of service to her. She took not the slightest notice of me and looked down on me contemptuously, as only a fly can do. Did she know about my case? But no—she had merely chosen this quiet spot so that she could devote herself for a few minutes undisturbed to her beauty routine, and when they are thus occupied ladies do not generally like to be disturbed. Nevertheless, I was not sufficiently gallant to look the other way: On the contrary, I watched her unceremoniously. And my little fly-maiden seemed to be thoroughly confident of her charm, for she let me watch without a word of objection and only once shrugged her shoulders briefly and disdainfully. She now delicately placed some of her legs under her glossy wings and carefully smoothed them, rather in the way a dancer smoothes her transparent ballet skirt—not, of course, using her legs. After she had convinced herself with a quick jerk of her remarkable head that her wings were perfect down to the last detail, she turned her attention assiduously to her feet, set about mani- and pedicuring them with a will, as if today she would have to infatuate a fly-baron or a filthy-rich bluebottle. The only thing I could not tell for sure, because of the inadequacy of the lighting, was whether she varnished her toe- and finger-nails blue or red. Once again she made this jerky move-ment with her head, and after she had given another swift polish to the third leg from the left, she turned to the application of her face make-up. I'm damned, I must admit, if I didn't actually start sweating with fear at her contortions, for I was afraid that at any moment she would twist her head out of its socket—and what good is a fly without a head? After she had energetically brushed back her short hair with the right front foot, she took her head between her two front legs and began to massage her neck, which was as slender as a knitting needle at any rate, so that I couldn't breathe for the suspense. But finally she had done that too and she went over to her eye treatment. After she had thoroughly brushed out her eyelashes she carefully pulled back her brows again, unable to resist as she did so the temptation to toss me a coquettish sideways glance. And then a tremor went through her body—apparently she was giving herself a final powdering all over—then she was ready, and then, pleased with herself, she strolled up and down just in front of my nose.

I don't know how it came about—but all this must have provoked me somehow. Is it a primitive, typically mascu-line characteristic, is it the hunter's instinct or is it just a reversion to the years of indiscretion? In any case, at

these challenging gestures of the fly my hand uncon-
sciously took up the familiar, distinctive position for
fly-catching and cautiously edged nearer to its apparently
unwitting victim. And then my reason began to issue some
explanatory thoughts. Perhaps it was seeking to justify
the peculiar behaviour of my hand. Anyway I thought:
Just as they have captured me, so I shall capture you now,
you tiny fly—I too shall play fate. I shall be your fate
and I shall at once decide between death and life. But I
got no further than thinking like that: For suddenly, as
my fateful hand was about to make a god-like grab it
struck empty space, it had been fooled—and the little
black inkspot was sitting as if nothing had happened only
a few centimetres higher up the wall, just high enough to
ensure that I couldn't reach it.

Resignedly I was about to fall back into my stupor
when the thought flashed through my mind like a hideous
nightmare: Didn't that fly just grin at me and nod indul-
gently at me with its stupid head? I was just about to
hurl my boot into the mocking face, when she spoke to
me—with a rather thin and very matter-of-fact voice
which did not, however, lack a certain practical wisdom—
she reminded me of my old scripture teacher. "You see,"
she said, "you wanted to be my fate and now I have eluded
you, you fool. One must stand above one's fate, even if
it's only by a few centimetres, precisely enough to ensure
that it cannot reach one and drag one down into the
depths. Do you understand that?"—"You have made a
laughing stock of me, fly," I raged up at her. "That's
just it," she answered coolly, "one must be able to smile
at one's fate. You see, you nincompoop, and then one
discovers that life is more of a comedy than a tragedy."
She struck an attitude, nodded at me once more briefly,
and then she was away, as suddenly as she had come.

I have pondered over it for ages and I have found that

the fly is right: One must stand above one's fate. I have often thought about my little fly who flew into my darkness like a tiny sunbeam, and as a sort of afterthought I have given her a name: I have called her Ching Ling. That is Chinese and means: The happy disposition.

15

MARY, IT'S ALL BECAUSE OF MARY

But when he took off his boots we could willingly have murdered him.

When he came into our cell it suddenly started smelling of animals and tobacco and sweat and fear and leather. He was a Pole. But he was as fair as any Teutonic type. And these flaxen-haired men were always rather insipid. He too. And what is more he was a bit shabby. He only knew a few words of German. But in his pocket he carried a beautiful, gaily coloured transfer-picture. He always used to pray to it for a very long time. He would prop it up against his beaker on his stool. He prayed in a loud voice and in Polish. The transfer-picture was edged with gold and was very colourful. It showed a girl with a red scarf and a blue dress. The dress was open. One breast could be seen. White. She was extremely thin. But she suited his purpose as someone to pray to. Maybe the white breast was there only as an accessory. In addition the girl had a few sun rays round her head. But otherwise she looked somewhat a dull person. Anyway, that's what we thought. But the Pole called her Mary. And as he did so he made a movement with his hand, as if he wanted to say: Well, isn't she just a beauty! But he probably intended to say something a little more tender when he grinned at us and said Mary. Perhaps it was meant to be a smile full of devotion, but we hated him so much that to us it was simply a grin. He said: Mary.

But when he took his boots off on that first evening we really felt like murdering him. It took him an hour: He had handcuffs on. It is hard to take your boots off when you've got handcuffs on. It is even worse when you have to scratch your face with handcuffs on. And then at night there were the bugs. And the Pole also had his "bracelets" on at night. He had been condemned to death. When the boots finally lay beside him a terrible smell permeated our cell. It crept up on us like an overpowering gypsy, impertinent, irresistible, sharp, hot and very strange. One cannot really call it altogether nasty. But we were at its mercy. It was overbearing and bestial. I looked at Liebig. The Pole sat between Paulus, Liebig and me on the floor. Liebig looked at me. "Poles," he said, and went back to staring out of the window. Liebig used to stand for weeks on end on tiptoes, staring out of the window. Three or four times a day he would say something. When the newcomer took his boots off Liebig said: "Poles." And he looked at me as if he were close to tears.

68

Gradually we got used to him. He smelled of Poland. (God knows what we smelled of!) But it took him an hour to take his boots off. That tried our patience. But after all he did have the handcuffs on. One couldn't kill him. He had to have the hour to take his boots off. In the evening when the sun made the window bars stroll across the ceiling. The bars were solid. But on the ceiling they looked like a spider's web. They were a spider's web. And in the evenings our cell reeked of Poland. It was ages since Liebig had said anything else. Only occasionally he would look across at me when the Pole was sitting between us on the floor. Then that was enough, too. And gradually we got used to him.

In return he cleaned out our bucket. Somebody had to do it. Paulus' fingers were too well looked after for such a job. Liebig just didn't do it. Mostly I had cleaned the bucket out. I had to talk myself into having the courage to do it. And with excuses like "everything is shit after all" or "work ennobles" I then got the better of myself. Now it was the Pole's job. I didn't know what sort of excuses he used. They must have been very effective for he got the bucket thoroughly clean, as we all agreed. He also quite enjoyed doing it for he hummed softly as he was working. Cheerful tunes from Poland. Thus we slowly got used to him, to his transfer-picture, his praying, his smell. We got used to Poland.

We even got used to his red foot-bandages. He had two marvellous red foot-bandages made of home-spun linen. As red as blackcurrant-groats. Every evening he carefully unwound them, folded them up, first the left, then the right, then put them one on top of the other and placed them on his straw bed at the head end. Then he went into the corner with his transfer-picture, propped it up against his beaker on his stool and prayed in a loud voice and in Polish. Then he grinned at each one of us and lay down.

69

Then he shoved his blackcurrant red foot-bandages under his head as a pillow. Of course that looked rather nice, the blond hair on the blackcurrant bandages. We could have murdered him when we saw him do that on that first evening for the first time. Liebig's mouth was already open ready to say "Poles," but then he changed his mind. Only his nostrils moved slightly. That was sufficient. But in time we also got used to the foot-bandages. And to the pillow.

When they came with the food tins he was just praying. Suddenly he turned his little pale face out of his corner towards us and shouted in the middle of his Mary-sing-song: "Marmalade!" We did not know what he meant. It could have been Polish. But then he sprang up, in a rage. He leapt up in Polish, pressed his porcelain dish into Liebig's hand and cried: "Marmalade! Marmalade! Please, for God's sake!"

Then he turned round, dropped to his knees and carried on praying. But then Liebig pushed him from behind. With his foot. And then Liebig made his longest speech in cell 432. To annoy the Pole he tried to mimic his accent. "What," shouted Liebig, "you miserable cripple, you! You arch-Masurian hog! You hypocrite, you. Marmalade, you shout, Marmalade? There we are, thinking you're praying and in seventh heaven with your flat-chested madonna! And all the time you've got your ears pricked to find out what's for eats, eh? All you can hear is marmalade, you greedy Polish sod!"

The Pole stood up. He said very gently and patiently: "What's the matter? One ear inside, one ear outside. Marmalade outside. Mary inside." And so saying he pressed the picture to his canvas suit. There, where his heart was.

Liebig said nothing. He gave me the marmalade dish. But he did not look at me. A quarter of an hour later they

70

unlocked the cells. There was coffee. There was bread. And today there was no cheese. There was marmalade.

But he carried on with Mary at night, too. At night the bugs would not let us sleep. And the women wouldn't, either, the emerald-eyed, cat-limbed women. The bugs had a sweet smell of marzipan when you squashed them. They smelled of fresh blood. The smell of women was long since faded. The women made us quiet at night. But the bugs made us curse until it grew light. Only the Pole did not curse. But one bright night I saw him holding his picture in his hand. And when we were stirring up all the filth in the world then he would say at the most "Mary, Mary," softly to himself. Towards dawn ducks sometimes used to rattle past on their way to the next canal, their wings making a rusty flapping noise. Then Liebig groaned every time, every time he groaned: "Man, what I'd give to be one of those ducks." And then everything was once more full of bugs and curses and women. Only the Pole then said under his breath: "Mary, Mary."

One night we were wakened by the grating of the door of our locker. It was the Pole. He was standing there, chewing. We knew for sure that he had eaten everything that evening. He always ate everything, every evening. Now he was standing there, chewing. Liebig leapt from his mattress and grabbed him by the hair. But before he could do anything the Pole said: "What are you trying to do? I am hungry." So Liebig let him go, lay down again and did not say another word. But half an hour later I could hear him cursing to himself. "Poles," he said. Nothing else.

But during the day we had trouble with him. Whenever hobnailed footsteps were heard at the end of our corridor the Pole quickly started his soft singsong. He had been condemned to death. Whenever a guard went past outside he was being taken away. Whenever the guard had gone

71

he had been reprieved. Until the next guard. He was taken away a thousand times every day. And a thousand times a day he was reprieved. For they were going past all day long. And, whenever one had passed, the Pole stopped his singsong, sighed and then looked at us and said: "Mary, it's all because of Mary." He said that as if to say; Well, you see, she always helps, she's a good girl. And he had to say that many times in a day, that bit about Mary, for they were going past all day long. And whenever they had gone past, he would always say calmly: "It's all because of Mary." And it sounded like: There you are, what did I tell you? And it drove us mad. And he grinned as he said it. But above his eyebrows was a line of sentries marching up and down: Little sparkling drops of water.

One day they did actually take him away. He was terrified. And he could not manage to grin. He just stood there, incredibly shocked. We could have murdered him.

In the middle of the night Liebig suddenly drew a sharp breath. Then he looked at the empty mattress. "I think it still smells of Poland," he said. And then he said: "And now he has gone away." Paulus and I said nothing. We knew that Liebig was sorry that he had hated the Pole.

Four months later I was released. I had to go down into the basement to the clothing store and get my things. The basement was just being scrubbed. Twenty prisoners were on their knees scrubbing the floor with steel wool, so that the corridor looked bright and friendly. Suddenly one of them tugged at my trousers. I looked down. It was the Pole. He grinned up at me.

"Pardoned," he whispered, "pardoned! Fifteen years, only fifteen years!" Then he beamed and stroked his breast pocket: "Mary," he whispered, "it's all because of Mary." And as he said this, he made a face, as if he had pulled a fast one over the judicial system. So he had. The judicial system of the whole world.

72

16

MARGUERITE

She was not pretty. But she was seventeen and I loved her. I really loved her. Her hands were always so cold, because she had no gloves. She didn't know her mother and she said: "My father is a swine." And she was born in Lyons.

One evening she said to me: "If the world should fall—*mais je ne crois pas*—then we will take a room, drink a lot of brandy and listen to music. Then we will turn on the gas and kiss each other until we are dead. I want to die in the arms of my darling, *ah oui!*"

Sometimes she also used to say *mon petit chou* to me. My little cabbage.

Once we were sitting in a café. The sound of the clarinet came hopping over to our corner like ten chickens. A woman was singing sensuous jazz and our knees found each other and were restless. We looked at each other. She laughed and I became so sad about it that she noticed at once. It had struck me—her laughter was so seventeen-year-old—that she would one day be an old woman. But I said that I was afraid that everything could come to an end. Then she laughed quite differently, softly: "Come."

The music had been so cosy that we felt the cold when we got outside and we had to kiss. It wasn't only the cold—it was also the jazz and the sadness.

Somebody interrupted us. It was a lieutenant and he had no face. Nose, mouth, eyes—they were all there, but it hardly added up to a face. But he wore a fine uniform and told us we couldn't kiss in broad daylight (and he emphasised that) on the street.

I got up and acted as if he were right. But he still did not go away.

Marguerite was furious: "Oh, can't we? Oh yes we can! We can, can't we?" She looked at me.

I was speechless and the uniform still didn't go away. I was afraid he would notice something, for Marguerite was extremely angry.

"But you! What kind of a man are you? Why, I wouldn't even kiss you in the middle of the night!"

Then he went away. I was happy. I had been scared stiff that he would notice that Marguerite was French. But it seems that officers don't really notice everything.

Then Marguerite's lips were once more on mine.

Once we were very angry with each other.

In the cinema the film showed the Paris Fire Brigade on parade. It was their jubilee. They marched in a down-right comical way. So I laughed. I should have thought before I did so. Marguerite stood up and moved to

74

another seat. It was clear that I had offended her. For half an hour I left her alone. Then I couldn't stand it any longer. The cinema was empty and I crept up unnoticed behind her:

"I love you. I love your hair, and your voice when you say *mon petit chou* to me. I love your language and all that is foreign about you. And your hands. Marguerite!"

And I thought that we probably submit to the charms of what is strange, because we find it so sweet when in the end we rediscover what is already familiar to us.

After the film Marguerite asked for my pipe. She smoked it and it made her sick. But she wanted to prove to me that she loved me even more.

We were standing by the river. It was black with night and lapped secretively against the pillars of the bridge. From time to time it glowed yellow and sporadic, rose and fell as if it were resting on a panting breast. Stars were reflected, yellow and sporadic.

We were standing by the river. But it sailed along with the night and did not drag us with it into an unknown land. Perhaps it, too, did not know where it was going and whether the destination of all journeying is paradise. Yet we would have entrusted ourselves unconditionally to the sailing of the night—but the river betrayed nothing to us of its magic. It lapped and gurgled and we sensed a little of its secretive beauty. For our sakes it could have stepped beyond its banks—and beyond ours, the banks of our life. This night we would have let ourselves be washed over, submerged.

We were breathing deeply and excitedly. And Marguerite whispered:

"It smells like love."

I whispered back:

"But surely it smells of grass, of water, river water and mist and night."

"Don't you see," whispered Marguerite again, "it also smells like love. Can't you smell it?"

"It smells like you," I whispered more softly, "and you smell like love."

"Don't you see?" she whispered once more.

Then the river whispered: "Like love—don't you see—like love—don't you see—"

Perhaps it meant something quite different. But Marguerite thought it had overheard us.

Suddenly the sound of footsteps grew closer to us and a lamp compelled us to close our eyes: Patrol!

They were looking for juvenile girls, for they blossomed like flowers in the parks in the arms of the soldiers. But Marguerite appeared adult enough to the patrol leader. We were just about to go when he noticed something about Marguerite. I think it was the style of her make-up. Our girls did not do it as she did. Sometimes sergeants are not as stupid as they look. He asked for her pass. She did not tremble in the least. "I thought as much!" he said. "Must be French, with a paint box like that!"

Marguerite remained quiet and I had to keep quiet too. Then he wrote down my name and we were alone again.

I knew I would not get out of the barracks for at least four weeks. Not to mention the other punishments. I waited a moment longer, but nothing better occurred to me. And I told Marguerite about it.

"You mean to say you won't come for four weeks? Oh, in that case it's all over, I know it. You're nothing but a coward. Am I a coward? Did I tremble? Fancy letting them lock you up for four weeks! Shame on you, you've got no courage! You don't love me. Oh, I know!"

It was no use. Marguerite thought I was just too much of a coward to climb over the fence every evening. She had no idea of the hundreds of little precautions taken to prevent such escapes. I thought about those four weeks and didn't know what else I could say. Then, after a while, she tried again:

"You're not coming? For four weeks? Really not?"

"I can't, Marguerite."

I couldn't think of anything else. And for Marguerite it was not enough.

"Well! Very well! Do you know what I shall do now?"

Of course, I did not know.

"Now I shall go to my room and wash my face. All of my face. Yes. Then I shall make myself pretty and look for a new lover. So! *Ah, oui.*"

Then she was swallowed up by the darkness, gone, finished—forever.

As I made my way alone back to the barracks I could have wept. I tried it. I held my hands in front of my face. They had a secret smell: France. And I thought that I would not wash my hands again that evening.

The tears just would not come. It was because of my boots. They grated wretchedly with every step I took:

Mon petit chou—my little cabbage—*mon petit chou.*

You giant cabbage, I grinned up at the moon. It was unashamedly bright. Otherwise the patrol would not have been able to notice it. Her make-up.

17

BEHIND THE WINDOWS
IT IS CHRISTMAS

∽◦∾

It's unbearable in the bunker. And when your face was lit up by the car I saw the blue shadows round your eyes. Perhaps she's one of the easier types, I thought. That's why I'm walking behind you.

The two of us are all alone in the city. Behind the windows it is Christmas. Sometimes you can see the candles on the Christmas tree near the window. I just couldn't stand it in the bunker, when they start singing. You have blue shadows under your eyes. Perhaps you are one of those who walk about in the evening. Those are shadows of love. But now they have changed, now they are singing Christmas carols and are ashamed because they can't help weeping. I left.

Do you have a room? And a Christmas tree? My God, if only you had a room! Have you noticed that I'm walking behind you? We are all alone in the city. And the street-lamps are standing guard. The guards have cigarettes, because today is Christmas, and they glow in the darkness. Can you hear? Behind the windows they are celebrating Christmas. They are sitting in soft chairs eating fried potatoes. Maybe they even have cabbage. But then, they are rich. But they have curtains, too, so they also have cabbage. Anyone who has curtains is rich. We are the only two who are outside. You have blue shadows beneath your eyes, I saw them when the car went past. I would like them to be shadows of love. But I do not know how else you could have got them. They are singing in the bunker. It's unbearable.

Whenever a streetlamp approaches I can see your legs. You can tell a lot by looking at legs. The others are always talking about the legs of their women. They always say women. When they come home in the evening they all talk about their women. Women, they always say. Always women, just like that. The whole hut is full of them when they talk about her legs, about her bust and her pink underwear.

Haven't you noticed that I am walking behind you all the time? Whenever a streetlamp approaches you always avert your head. I suppose I'm too small for you, is that it? Yes, all at once I am too small. I was not too small for the war. Only for something nice. You need not hurry like that, I'll still follow you. When I think of all the other things you have, apart from your legs, well, it's easy to imagine all sorts of things. The others have it every evening. Under the streetlamps your knees are very

79

white. Whenever I catch up with you at a streetlamp you always avert your face.

When I go past I can smell you. But you don't even notice that I want to get to know you. You won't get rid of me that quickly. In any case, I don't know where I'm heading for. When the weather is foggy like this it is always cold and damp in the bunker. It may be that you have a room. At least, not in your parents' house. With friends. Then you can take me with you. Then we can sit side by side on your bed. And the fog and the cold can stay outside. And then your white knees will be pressed up close to me. And you have a Christmas tree. And then we will share a piece of bread. You're bound to have some bread. The others always tell how they get something to eat from their women. You lot don't eat as much as we do. We are usually hungry most of the time. So am I, let me tell you. But maybe you have something to eat. If you live with your parents it messes everything up. Then we will have to stay outside on the staircase. Even that would be something. The others often stay outside on the staircase with their women. But Christmas? My God! On the staircase.

You smell good. I am walking right up close behind you and I can smell you. My God, you smell of all kinds of things. It conjures up all kinds of things. If only the lads in the bunker could smell like you. But there it always smells of tobacco and leather and wet kitbags. You smell so different; I've never smelt anything like you before. At the next streetlamp I will talk to you. The street just happens to be completely empty. But if I talk to you it might mean the end of everything. Maybe you won't even answer. Or you might laugh at me because I am too young for you. But you are no older than twenty yourself.

There's the streetlamp. Your knees are so bright in the

gloom. The streetlamp is coming. Now I must say something at once. Or not yet? Perhaps it will all be finished.
All the others can do it. They've all got their women.
There's the streetlamp. If I speak now everything might
be over. The streetlamp. No, I'll wait a few more street-
lamps. Not yet. The fog is good. At least you can't see
that I am not very old. But I know some who've got one
and they're no older. Yes, now I am too small again, all
of a sudden. Not too small to be a soldier. And now I'm
running round. On a foggy night. And every evening
the others talk about their women. Afterwards it's
impossible to get to sleep because of it. Then the air in
the bunker is full of it. Of their women. And of the
foggy wet night. Outside. But you, you smell good.
Your knees are so bright in the darkness. I bet they're
nice and warm, those knees of yours. When the next
streetlamp comes I shall talk to you. Perhaps something
will come of it. Woman, you really do smell nice. I've
never smelled anything like it. Just look, behind the
curtains it's Christmas for them. Maybe cabbage, too.
Only the two of us are outside. We are all alone in the
city.

18

THE PROFESSORS KNOW
NOTHING EITHER

I am an omelette. Maybe not so appetising and crispy, but at least I lie just as yellow and flat in the black mood of my illness as an omelette in the black bottom of its frying pan. My liver is a bouncing football and my head is a glowing teapot. The rest, between the football and the teapot is sore and swollen like an appendix.

It was a genius who thought up the word malaria. I reckon it comes from *mal*, as in *malodorous*, and *airy*— light and floating: That's just how I feel: bad, airy, like an omelette.

Beside me something is hammering on the table—

and has been doing so for a few hours. On a chair at the table sit ninety pounds hammering away at the forty-five pounds standing on the table.

The forty-five pounds on the table—that is my big, heavy typewriter. The ninety pounds sitting at the table—that is my light, thin father. For hours my father has been tapping an insane rhythm on the machine and every beat is the beat of an infernal machine and the infernal machine is my head.

But outside there are birds, cars and grey clouds, which really must get to the laundry this evening because they are as dirty as the towels in the public conveniences. Yet the birds know that behind the towels the sky is still blue—well, and the cars are honking all right. Whoever honks must be healthy. Birds, towels and horns annoy me because I can't join in, because I'm ill: tap—tap— bang—bang.

But I am making every effort to be patient, like a martyr whose fingernails are being burned off and who wants to please God with his angelic patience. (What sort of people these angels must have been! And as for God. . . !)

My dear, attentive ninety pounds thrust through the heavy machine what my teapot head has brewed— which explains my saintly patience. In fact, at night, when my football liver is coughing bacteria through my veins, then my insomniac teapot-like head brews stories— and my father writes them down in the morning.

My father weighs ninety pounds and the machine forty-five pounds, but he insists that it does him good. The truth of the matter is merely that he is afraid that if he didn't do it I would torture myself out of my frying-pan blackness and start tapping away myself. He knows that I would not be able to rest, so he spends hours enacting my reveries on the machine—ninety pounds against forty-five! That's terrible, absolutely terrible!

But he is my father and he is frightened that my liver would swell to the size of a Zeppelin and my head would turn into a turbine and both might—because of inadequate ventilation—somehow explode. Therefore he acts as my ventilator, my father, in order to prevent the development of both turbine and Zeppelin, for who can tell? Maybe somebody with spectacles? What use are spectacles if there is nothing behind them, nothing but a disdainful smile and eyes filled with tears that are not withheld out of wisdom but out of stupidity. One must always distinguish between the two: the silence of wisdom and the silence of stupidity. I prefer to renounce the bespectacled celebrities—no, the professors know nothing either.

My father knows—about my not getting any rest and about my liver, because he is my father—and so he struggles with the forty-five pounds.

Then we quarrel. The ninety pounds against the dry cough and the omelette-coloured teapot-like head, my father and I.

In my story I tell how the bone of a cat surfaces anaemically from the mud of a canal. The bone of a cat? Oh, my father is not satisfied with that. He poses the bluntest questions:

"How do you know that it is the bone of a cat that's lying there in your canal and, what's more, casts off the dead weight of eternity to emerge anaemically?"

I am surprised, but quite certain. I just know it. Only cats are drowned in canals. And besides, I know it.

But the ninety pounds are not so easily intimidated: amongst others, the following drown in canals—dogs, sparrows, rotten fish, old antlers, strangled bankers, pleasure girls murdered while being raped, and love-sick

84

third formers. Cats, too, of course—but no professor of anatomy, who is in any case usually shortsighted, would be able to tell from a bridge whether it was the bone of a cat or of a pleasure girl—after all, professors know nothing, either, old chap.

Aha! My father becomes the writer and the son of my father is looking for an easy way out. I know it was the bone of a cat, I know it for certain. If I write that it was the bone of a cat then it was the bone of a cat come what may, and that's that. Anyone who rejects my story on account of the bone of a cat can do so as far as I'm concerned! I'm not bothered about such pedantic readers. It was the bone of a cat, don't you see? What else?

Then, from the other side of the table, quite gently: "How about writing: It was the skeleton of a cat—a skeleton?"

And I, convinced, but too miserable to admit it: "Very well, then, for your sake, a skeleton."

In the doorway stands a tall, dark girl—no, a fair girl. She has dark eyes and dark hair but she brings more light than seven suns into my black mood.

My father sniffs and goes—he knows that otherwise I would get a liver like a Zeppelin—to my mother in the kitchen. He has sniffed and goes and knows that it will be cold and unfriendly in the kitchen. But he goes—he knows that I can do without his pale moonlight when the dark girl is there—who is a sun to me.

In the kitchen he will spend at least forty minutes arguing with my mother the illogicality of the cat's bone—oh, I know that with more certainty than I ever knew the dates of Napoleon's battles—I know it, see it and hear it. And I know that a pig's bone would please my mother better, then she would not have to worry about her ninety-pound husband.

Around her shoulders my mother wears gipsy-like a red and blue spotted shawl, which is held in place by a rustic clasp. I can see them now in the kitchen, sharing a cigarette and throwing the cat's bone into the canal again—attached to a skeleton. That is what it is like at the moment in our kitchen. Anyway, I saw it quite clearly, too clearly.

But then I see nothing more—how on earth can I? The dark girl has now thrown her coat over a chair and sits down beside me. Her nineteen years make my pulse race like a monkey up a palm tree, from where it throws coconuts down to me.

"Is that your heart?"

"No, coconuts—yes, it is my heart, because you are there, my sun."

I forget the kitchen, the cat's bone and the coconuts and my sun has to put up with the fact that I stare speechlessly and intently at her—without going blind.

She attempts to feel my pulse—is that what she wanted? —but the monkey has gone and I hold her hand tightly. Outside, the towels are now being wrung out. Birds and cars are emitting, partly dejectedly offended, partly enragedly pompous sounds. As far as I am concerned it can rain for three weeks, for the sun is sitting not a hand's breadth away from me—I can feel her back against my shinbone—I am almost as fit as a fiddle. What do I care about cars and birds now!

In the meantime we suddenly realise, as a result of a few barely audible words, that we like each other. It isn't the words that make us realise.

"Were your ears ringing yesterday evening?"

"Yesterday evening? Yours must be ringing all the time."

No, it was not that. It was the tone of our voices that made us realise (sometimes we use this tone with very young animals—like this—like the way in which we spoke).

The monkey—hey! What strength the fellow has!— unleashes a concentrated barrage of coconuts. But not only at me. For the fair dark girl suddenly looks at me disquieted. On her neck a tiny bit of blue vein is quivering.

We are both so wise or so stupid—or so surprised—that neither of us speaks. What were we even supposed to say? Run to all the libraries in the world, seek out all the love stories in the world and you will not find one even remotely sensible sentence that could have been used at this moment.

Brandy and fever imbue courage. I have no brandy but I do have a fever. And I become rash.

I shove the hand of my sun under my shirt to my heart.

"Can you hear it? A monkey is sitting there smashing coconuts. Coconuts, millions of big fat coconuts. More and more, faster and faster! Can you feel it?"

Then she says very softly.

"Oh, yes—here: the same is happening to me, too."

Then neither of us say anything else. What else is there to say? No tenor in the world would sound any better after our coconuts. Nobody could experience anything more beautiful. Certainly not the professors. The professors know nothing at all!

But my father knows that the machine-gun barrage of coconuts would ruin my liver if he did not intervene. So he comes—the cat's bone long since forgotten—out of the kitchen, and sits down behind the machine. He is my father and he knows that two hours of sunshine are quite ample for an invalid, and my good, dear sun also realises it suddenly: A pity!

The monkey slides down from his palm tree, blissfully tired, and the dark girl says: "— soon, of course, bye, bye—" when I ask her when she will be standing in my doorway again.

Then with the tinny rhythm of the typewriter, my father taps me into a dream of paradise. It is dream of palm trees, coconuts, monkeys, and dark, dark eyes.